Papa's Book of Mormon Christmas

BONNEVILLE BOOKS
AN IMPRINT OF CEDAR FORT, INC.
SPRINGVILLE, UTAH

Written by EMMA RAE PARKER ❄ Illustrated by ALEXA TERRY HANSON

"Tell me a story," Alice said. She broke off an icicle and plopped it in her mouth.

"'Twas the night before Christmas . . ."

"I heard that one already, Papa," she said with her tongue stuck to the ice.

Papa smiled as Alice wiggled her tongue loose.

She jumped from one snow pile to the next, yelling "Christmas, Christmas! I love Christmas!" as white mist puffed up around her. "Papa, can you hardly wait to play with all our toys tomorrow? I hope you were as good as I was this year."

Papa laughed. "I wasn't nearly that good."

Alice shook her head. She thought he would have learned by now. If he wasn't careful, he'd find himself a muddy pair of used shoes under the tree. Or worse, a slice of her daddy's fruitcake.

"Have you heard the story about the book that saved Christmas?" Papa asked.

Alice widened her eyes as big as oranges and shook her head no.

"Long ago, my papa wanted to buy his family a book."

"Papas have papas?" Alice asked with a wrinkled nose.

"The book took years and years to make. It was the most important book in the world."

"Better than *Peter Rabbit*?"

Alice lay down in the snow and spread her arms wide like an angel.

"This book was different," Papa said as he collected a handful of snow. "This book was for families and made people feel happy. This book took a lot of work and hard times to make so that everyone could read it. Finally, on Christmas Day, my papa brought the book home as a gift!"

He set the snow down and began rolling another snowball.

"Couldn't he bring toys home for Christmas too?" Alice raised her eyebrows with worry as she imagined a toyless Christmas.

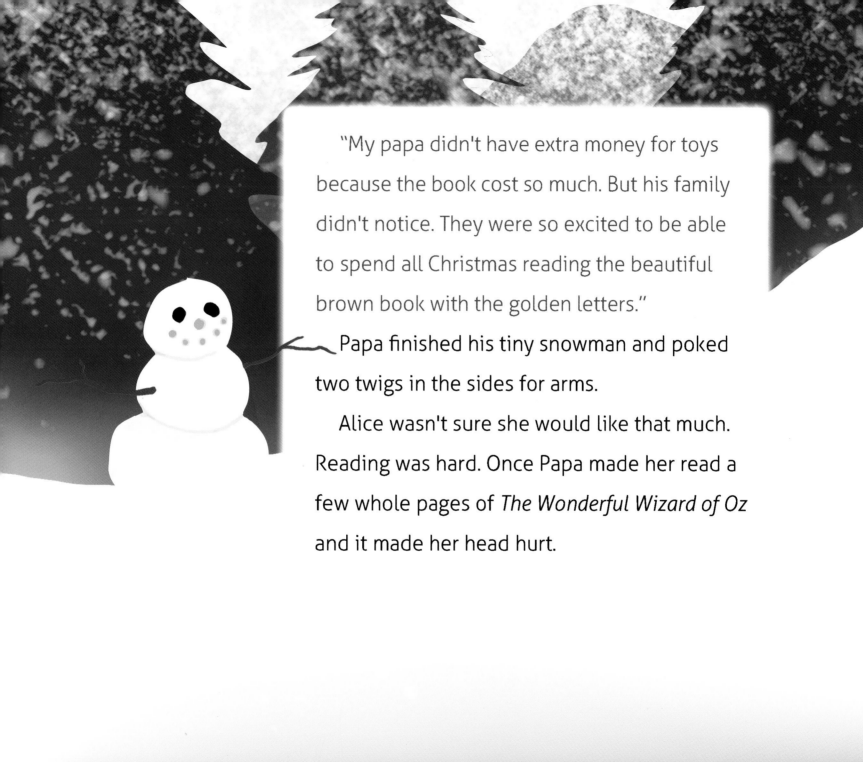

"My papa didn't have extra money for toys because the book cost so much. But his family didn't notice. They were so excited to be able to spend all Christmas reading the beautiful brown book with the golden letters."

Papa finished his tiny snowman and poked two twigs in the sides for arms.

Alice wasn't sure she would like that much. Reading was hard. Once Papa made her read a few whole pages of *The Wonderful Wizard of Oz* and it made her head hurt.

"I think I would want a jump rope and paint brushes instead." Alice watched as the crooked man of snow toppled over.

Papa smiled at Alice's chattering teeth. "Let's go inside. Santa is on his way, and his cookies won't frost themselves!"

Alice jumped up and ran toward the house. The sugary smell of warm cookies greeted her as she bounced inside and pulled off her coat.

"What colors do you want, Little Angel?" Papa asked as he walked into the kitchen.

Alice hopped on a stool and, on her tip-top toes, peeked at the cookies on the counter.

Papa tied an apron around the tiny girl.

"Green and pink!" Alice said.

"Don't tell me you're going to make Santa's suit pink."

Alice squeezed her eyes shut and gave him a goofy smile. She smeared some pink frosting all over the chubby man-shaped cookie. "How did the golden book save Christmas?"

Papa spread green frosting on a tree-shaped cookie. "When I was young, I read the book with my papa every day. Then I got a letter that said I had to join the war."

"I had to leave my family and fight in my own country."

"Were you sad?" Alice poured some sprinkles on a reindeer cookie.

"I knew I was doing the right thing. We fought for all people to be free and to be treated nicely. But I missed my family."

"Were you all alone?" Alice looked up from her frosting.

"Not so alone," he said, smiling. "Before I left, my papa gave his old book to me."

"The one with the shiny letters?" she squeaked.

"It was the best present ever. It helped me feel close to my family during the whole war."

Alice felt tingly as she imagined the gold-lettered book. She almost felt like someone had wrapped a fluffy blanket around her.

"When Christmas came, I really needed the book's comfort," Papa said.

"What happened?"

"There was an attack on Christmas Eve, and I lost my unit of soldiers. I was alone and lost and sad that the war was making brothers fight against brothers. That night, as I hid in a cold, creaky building, I pulled out my papa's gold-lettered book. As I read under a blanket, I met Nephi!"

"Who's that?" Alice pointed her spoon at Papa and flung pink frosting at him. They laughed.

"Nephi had to fight against his brothers too. He only wanted to do what God asked. But his brothers didn't understand. They were mean to him and even tied him to a boat!"

Alice was about to take a bite of her cookie but dropped it.

"How mean!"

"Nephi always loved his brothers anyway. All day that Christmas as I searched for my fellow soldiers, when I needed company, I would reach in my bag and read the book with gold letters."

"You had a new friend named Nephi." Alice smiled.

Papa nodded. "It turned out to be a pretty good Christmas."

Alice sighed as Papa tucked her in that night. "Papa, can you read me the Christmas book with shiny letters soon?"

Papa smiled as Alice closed her eyes. "Maybe very soon."

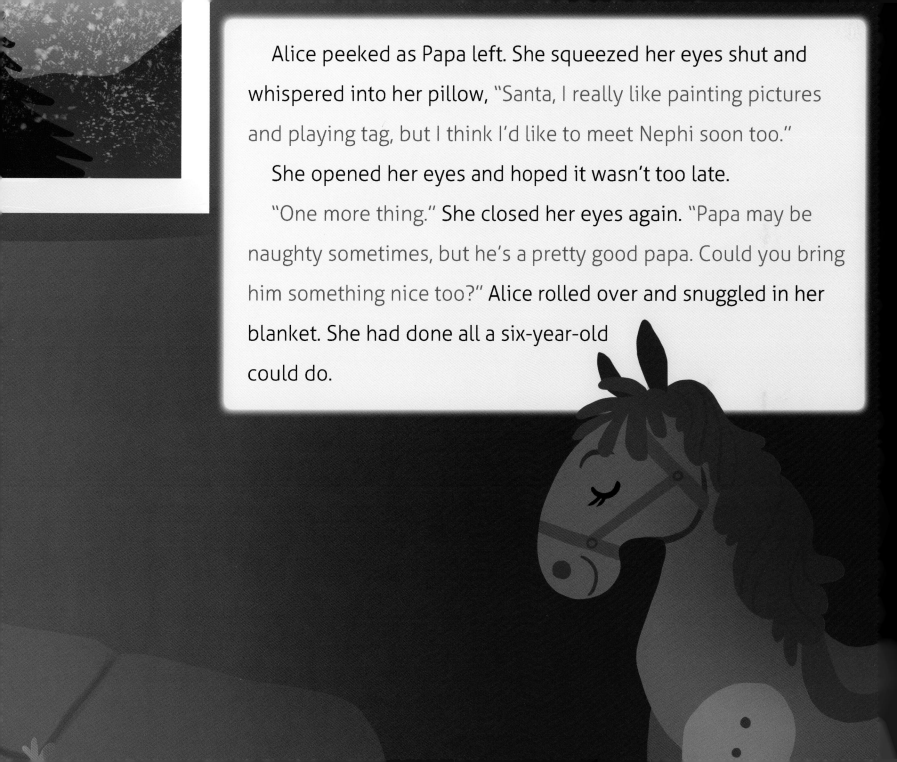

Alice peeked as Papa left. She squeezed her eyes shut and whispered into her pillow, "Santa, I really like painting pictures and playing tag, but I think I'd like to meet Nephi soon too."

She opened her eyes and hoped it wasn't too late.

"One more thing." She closed her eyes again. "Papa may be naughty sometimes, but he's a pretty good papa. Could you bring him something nice too?" Alice rolled over and snuggled in her blanket. She had done all a six-year-old could do.

The next morning, Alice ripped off the jingle-belled paper from her papa's Christmas gift. She gasped as shiny gold letters appeared that read: The Book of Mormon.

The tree's twinkle lights gleamed in the tears collecting in Alice's eyes. "Papa, the Christmas book!"

Her new jump rope and paint kit lay alone on the floor the rest of the day as Alice cuddled on the couch with Papa and her new book.

THE
END

© 2015 Emma Rae Parker
Illustrations © 2015 Alexa Terry Hanson

ISBN 13: 978-1-4621-1741-3

Published by Bonneville Books, an imprint of Cedar Fort, Inc.,
2373 W. 700 S., Springville, UT 84663
Distributed by Cedar Fort, Inc., www.cedarfort.com

LIBRARY OF CONGRESS CATALOGING-IN-PUBLICATION DATA

Parker, Emma Rae.
  Papa's Book of Mormon Christmas / Emma Rae Parker.
      pages cm
  Summary: Spending Christmas holidays with her grandfather, Papa, Alice listens as he tells the story of the Book of Mormon that he received as a Christmas present long ago.
  ISBN 978-1-4621-1741-3 (hardback : alk. paper)
  1. Christmas stories. [1. Christmas--Fiction. 2. Grandfathers--Fiction. 3. Book of Mormon--Fiction.] I. Title.
  PZ7.1.P364Pap 2015
  [E]--dc23

  6748

2015011907

Cover and Page design by Michelle May
Cover design © 2015 by Lyle Mortimer
Edited by Justin Greer

Printed and bound in China

10 9 8 7 6 5 4 3 2 1

Printed on acid-free paper

To Mom; to Dad—the Papa in mind; to all my tinies—who think this story is about them; and to Jared—you're the world's best sport and make me feel pretty stellar.

—Emma

For my parents, Steve and Belinda Terry, as well as my husband, Mike Hanson. Without their support during times when I felt down, I wouldn't have had the confidence in my talents to put my name out there.

— Alexa